This book belongs to

{ .... }

This book is dedicated to

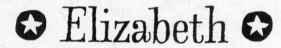 Elizabeth

(a really rather remarkable girl)

First published in paperback in Great Britain by HarperCollins Children's Books in 2010

1 3 5 7 9 10 8 6 4 2

ISBN: 978-0-00-733739-2

HarperCollins Children's Books is a division of HarperCollins Publishers Ltd.

Text and illustrations copyright © Tom Percival 2010

Visit our website at: www.harpercollins.co.uk

Printed in China

TOBIAS
☠ AND THE ☠
SUPER SPOOKY GHOST BOOK

TOM PERCIVAL

HarperCollins *Children's Books*

Tobias didn't have many friends.
In fact, he didn't have any.

"Perhaps it's because I'm a ghost?"
he wondered sadly.

He knew lots of other ghosts...

But they were all so old, and so very,

very BORING,

especially Great Uncle Finnegan.

So Tobias hung around the empty old house, bored and all alone.

Outside the world was changing,

but for Tobias, everything stayed the same.

Then something happened
that would change his afterlife forever...
A young couple moved in
with their daughter, Eliza.

The grown-ups thought the creepy old house had 'potential'. Eliza thought that it probably had rats!

"At last," chuckled Tobias. "Time for some fun!"

Late that night, a mysterious voice woke Eliza.

Where was it coming from, and who could it be?

Tobias burst out as if from nowhere!
Eliza screamed!
"Scared you!" cackled Tobias,
before he whooshed away.

"You horrid little ghost!" shouted Eliza.
"You won't scare me again!"

But he did!
Tobias waited until the whole house fell silent,
then he rounded up his most fearsome bats.

With a fluttering of leathery wings, the ghastly group
burst into Eliza's bedroom.

Poor Eliza was terrified!

Back in the attic, Tobias cackled with glee. Then something interesting caught his eye...

It was Great Uncle Finnegan's

SUPER SPOOKY GHOST BOOK.

There were more tricks in that old book
than Tobias could have ever imagined.

He decided to try one out there and then.

But it's hard to see where you're going with your head tucked under your arm…

As the little ghost tumbled down the stairs, his head flew one way and the book went another!

When he was finally back in one piece,
Tobias felt very silly and stomped off to his room.

But he'd forgotten about something important...
the **SUPER SPOOKY GHOST BOOK!**

Eliza flicked through the magical book in wonder. "That nasty little ghost won't know what's hit him!" she smirked.

Meanwhile, Tobias was busy practising his new trick.

"Get ready for the fright
of your life!"
he grinned as he crept
up behind Eliza.

"Not this time!" laughed Eliza
as she cast the scariest, spookiest,
most spine-chilling spell
in the whole book.

It was Tobias's turn
to be terrified!

But Eliza couldn't stop the spell and now the whole house was filling with monsters!

"What shall we do?" she panicked.
"RUN!" squealed Tobias.

They dashed this way…

And that way…

But nowhere was safe.

"HELP!"

they yelled.

In a crackling flash, Great Uncle Finnegan
appeared, larger than life and fiercer than fury.
"DEMONS, BE GONE!" he boomed.

And two seconds later, they were! Except now there was a new problem…

Great Uncle Finnegan was NOT happy.
"You foolish pair!" he scolded. "I hope you've learnt your lesson? Now, get this mess tidied up!"

"This will take forever," sighed Eliza.
"Maybe not," winked Tobias.

There was a flash of ghostly magic
as he whisked all the mess away.

Eliza gasped in wonder.
"Oh, that's nothing!" boasted Tobias.
"Do you want to see some more tricks?"

"Maybe…"
said Eliza cautiously,
"but only if you **STOP** trying to scare me!"
So Tobias showed Eliza
all of his favourite tricks.

The funny ones…

The silly ones…

But none of the scary ones!

And the spooky fun didn't stop until sunrise.

"I'm sorry I scared you," said Tobias. "I was just bored."

"That's OK," said Eliza. "We can be friends,

but no more tricks, OK?"

"I'd like that," said Tobias.

"I promise I'll never scare you again..."

"Well," he grinned, "Maybe just sometimes…"